Harpies

by

David Belbin

Published in Great Britain by Barrington Stoke Ltd
10 Belford Terrace, Edinburgh EH4 3DQ
Copyright © 2001 David Belbin
First published in different form in *Haunting Time* (Five
Leaves Publications, 1998)

ISBN 1-84299-031-4
Printed by Polestar AUP Aberdeen Ltd

A Note from the Author

I visited Crete on holiday and went to all of the places which appear in this book. I must have heard the legend of the Harpies at the same time.

A lot of writers get turned on by myths and legends. I don't. I like to make up my own stuff, not borrow characters from the great stories of the past. But then one day something clicked in my head.

Legends change with each new storyteller. The teller changes the tale for each new audience. My *Harpies* started out as a long story – now it is a short novel.

I'd like to thank the many readers who offered comments on the manuscript. Their names are listed at the back of this book.

For Ross Bradshaw

Contents

Chapter 1

The Disco

That August, the Greek islands were incredibly hot. It was so hot on Crete that when tourists tried to make the short walk into the city, many collapsed before they'd got halfway.

The Cooper family were staying on the edge of Heraklion. The city was an ugly, sprawling, modern mess. Cassie Cooper wished that they were staying some place else, maybe Agios Nikolaos, where the discos didn't stop till dawn.

At least their hotel had its own disco. It took place in the basement beneath the dining room. The disco was open to anyone but hotel guests didn't have to pay. Cassie's second night at the hotel was a Saturday. She got to the disco early and sat at a table with a good view. Then she waited for the evening to get going.

Most of the people who came in were at least twenty. Cassie felt out of place. She looked her age, which was fifteen. Older boys floated towards her and didn't seem to like what they saw. She was too young, too skinny or too lonely looking. Cassie looked around for her older brother, Ben. He'd promised to join her later.

That was when she saw them. The three girls came out of the lift and made straight for the dance floor. The first was Becky's age.

She was well-dressed but dumpy, with short, brown hair. The second girl was sixteen or seventeen. She was thin, with long blonde hair, like a model from a shampoo advert. The third was nineteen or twenty and nearly six feet tall with jet black hair and a full figure.

"Excuse me?" The speaker was Paul, a shy, black teenager from Southport. He was on holiday with his mate Darren. Cassie had met the two of them at the disco the day before. Darren had already paired off with a German girl.

"Would you l-like ...?" Paul stammered.

"Sure," Cassie said.

Paul was a bad talker but a good dancer. The evening was looking up. As they walked onto the dance floor, Cassie pointed out the three girls.

"They just came out of the lift. I'm sure they're not staying here. I bet they sneaked in without paying. Have you seen them before?"

Paul shook his head. "The blonde one sure is beautiful," he said.

Cassie gritted her teeth. He was meant to tell her how pretty *she* was, not stare at another girl as though Cassie wasn't there. While they danced, Paul kept looking at the three girls. When the track ended, Cassie decided she had had enough.

"Thanks for the dance, Paul."

She left him standing on the dance floor and went to look for her brother. No Ben. She saw that Paul was talking to two of the new girls. There was a gap in the music. Cassie heard the girls tell Paul their names. The tall, dark one was Carla. The blonde was Alice. Paul began to dance with her. There was no sign of the third girl, the dumpy one.

4

Cassie sat down at her table. Most of the other tables were empty. There were several kissing couples, including Paul's mate Darren and his German girlfriend. A strobe light began to flash. At one table, Cassie spotted the dumpy girl. Then she was gone. A moment later, she was back again, but at a different table. What was going on? Maybe it was the strobe light, confusing Cassie.

Cassie decided to take a closer look. She walked between the tables, as if she was heading for the loo. What was that bump in the curtains? It seemed to be moving. Cassie was about to look behind the curtain when the lift door opened. Her brother stepped out.

Ben was eighteen, tall and handsome. He had just finished his A levels. If he got the right results, he'd be going to Leeds University in a couple of months.

"Having fun?" he asked.

Cassie shook her head.

"Dance one with me then."

A moment later, they were dancing. Cassie looked around for Alice and Carla, wanting to show off her handsome partner. But the girls and Paul from Southport were gone.

Chapter 2
Thieves

At breakfast the next morning, the gossip was everywhere. Last night, at the disco, several purses and wallets had been stolen. Cigarette lighters, mobiles and other small items had also been taken.

"The hotel manager swore to me that it had never happened before," one woman told the whole room. "But that doesn't bring back Vicki's thousand drachmas, does it?"

"It seems you were lucky not to lose anything last night," Dad told Ben and Cassie.

Cassie didn't reply. From her point of view, the evening had been a write off. Quietly, she told Dad about the dumpy girl, who she was sure was behind the thefts. Dad told the hotel manager, who wrote down a description of the girl.

"I don't think anyone like that is staying in the hotel," he said.

It was as Cassie had suspected. The three girls had used the hotel lift to sneak in without paying. Cassie looked around to see if she could spot Paul from Southport. She wondered if he'd had anything stolen. Darren was at breakfast, but there was no Paul. Maybe he was sleeping in.

Later, the Coopers took a bus to see some ruins in the middle of the island. The sun blazed. Dad's bald spot began to burn, turning from pink to a violent red. Cassie and Mum wore wide-brimmed straw hats. Ben had borrowed a New York Yankies baseball cap from Cassie. It didn't suit him.

The ruins went on forever. Mum, Dad and Cassie went round them, trailing behind a group with a guide. Ben wandered around on his own. Cassie tried to pick out her brother from the crowd, but it was hard. The ruins were very crowded with lots of people wearing a baseball cap and sunglasses. The Coopers kept having to wait for large parties to move on before they could get near a ruin. A loud American was asking a question.

"What about the treasures that were here? Where did they go?"

"Stolen," the guide replied. "Used for trade. But also, around here, there is a legend." He pointed to the mountains around them. "Spirits live in the hills. They take things and fill secret caves with their treasure."

"What are these spirits called?" Cassie asked.

"We call them *Harpies*. They are big, cruel, very ugly birds. Some people say they have the faces of women. They are dangerous spirits, thousands of years old."

Then the guide went on to explain that the Harpies were Greek gods. They arrived in a fierce wind. They would pounce, then snatch anything they could take, especially people. Because of this, their sister, the goddess Iris, had banished them to a cave in these mountains.

Cassie was about to ask another question, but Mum poked her with an elbow. "He'll want paying if you keep asking questions," she said. "Have you seen Ben? We don't want to lose all sight of him."

Cassie looked around. She couldn't see her brother, but she could see Carla, the tall, dark-haired beauty from last night. She wore no hat and a simple, sleeveless dress. If she wasn't careful, she would get terrible sunburn. But where was Ben? Cassie kept looking. Now she saw the dumpy girl from the night before. She was moving quickly through the crowd. Every now and then, she paused. What was she up to? Maybe she was picking pockets?

The Cooper family kept on walking. It was too hot to take much interest in the ruins. Cassie wished that she was swimming or sunbathing. This was too much like hard work.

"There he is!" Mum said.

And there was Ben, walking up the hill towards them. But he wasn't alone. He was arm in arm with the tall, dark Carla.

And Carla was wearing Cassie's baseball cap!

"Who's that he's with?" Dad asked.

Carla took her arm out of Ben's. She let her hand glide down his arm and whispered something. Then she kissed him on the cheek before turning away. A moment later, Carla was lost in the crowd. She was still wearing Cassie's baseball cap.

"Who was that pretty girl we saw you with?" Mum asked Ben, on the bus back to Heraklion.

"What girl?" Ben was putting on an act.

"The tall girl in the sleeveless dress who kissed you goodbye," Mum said, teasingly.

"Oh," Ben mumbled. "Her."

"Yes. Her."

"She fainted," Ben explained. "From the heat. I was standing nearby and caught her. I took her into the shade until she felt better. Then I lent her your cap, Cassie."

"That's my favourite cap! Grandad got it for me!"

"Sorry. I thought you'd understand."

"Understand?" Cassie said. "All I understand is that you've given my cap to some girl who you'll probably never see again."

"I'm seeing Carla tonight, as it happens," Ben replied. "She's staying near our hotel."

"Do you really think a girl like her is interested in you?" Cassie asked.

"Why not?" Ben challenged her.

"That's enough!" Dad said. "Cassie, I'm sure you'll get your cap back tonight."

Ben didn't talk to Cassie for the rest of the journey. She felt bad about getting at her brother.

Ben was good looking but shy. He'd never had a serious girlfriend. Carla was at least two years older than him. Also, she was gorgeous. Way too good for Ben. No way could she be interested in Cassie's brother.

Chapter 3

Two Boys

That evening, at dinner, there were four new arrivals. Nick Smith was about sixteen. He had fair hair, blue eyes and a square jaw. He was there with his parents and his friend Callum was on holiday with him. Callum was the same age as Nick, with wavy brown hair and kind eyes.

Cassie fancied him at once. She spent ages getting ready for the disco that night. The two boys were bound to be there.

That night was when the holiday really took off. Cassie danced with each boy in turn. In between dances, they talked about music, videos, computer games and her holiday so far. At one point, Cassie told them about the three girls from the night before and the things that had gone missing.

"Are you sure they're thieves?" Callum asked.

"No. Only the dumpy one. At least I suspect she is."

"And the tall, dark one took your baseball cap?" Nick asked.

"Sort of," Cassie replied. She realised that the story sounded rather petty. "My brother lent it to her."

"And there's a third girl, isn't there?" Callum said. "What does she look like?"

"Alice is very pretty," Cassie told him. "She's got long, blonde hair. The other night

16

she was dancing with a boy I know." Cassie hadn't seen Paul since, she realised. What had happened to him?

"We'll keep an eye out for them," Callum promised.

"Good," Cassie said. "Now let's talk about something else."

"How about another dance?" Nick suggested.

While Cassie was dancing, she saw her brother. Ben was waiting near the disco entrance looking forlorn. Carla hadn't shown up.

The boys' curfew was half past eleven. They took Cassie to her door. Cassie was excited. She tried to decide which boy she liked best. Nick was better looking and had more to say than Callum. But Callum was kind, gentle, more her type. It didn't matter.

They were both good company. But she might have trouble separating them.

At midnight, there was a light tap on her door. Cassie thought it would be her parents, who'd been out drinking in a city bar. But it was Ben.

"You were right about Carla," he said. "She didn't show up. I'm sorry about your cap. I'll get you another one."

"Forget it," Cassie told him. "I'm sorry she let you down."

Outside, after the hot, still day, a fierce wind blew.

Chapter 4
In The Park

The next day, the Cooper family went shopping in Heraklion. The city was very crowded and very hot. Soon, all four of them were tired. Luckily, they found a small park with benches and shady trees. In the middle of the park was a statue of the painter, El Greco, who was born nearby. The park was named after him.

The four rested in the park and each had an ice cream. Then Dad went off to buy tickets for a day trip to the other side of the island. Cassie and Mum wanted to look for clothes. Ben said he'd wait for them in the park. He wanted to read his book in the shade.

When Cassie and her Mum got back to El Greco Park, Dad was there, alone. They waited for Ben. And waited. And waited.

An hour passed before Cassie's brother strolled back into the park. His face had a glow which Cassie hadn't seen before. "I hope you haven't been waiting long," he said, with a bright smile. "I met Carla."

"Who?" Mum asked.

"The girl from yesterday. She came into the park just after you left. We went for a drink."

"Did she have my cap?" Cassie asked

"No, but I'm meeting her at the Beach Bar tonight. She'll bring your cap then."

On the bus back to the hotel, Mum began to quiz Ben about Carla. "Where's she from, this girl? Is she English?"

"Half-American. Half-Greek, too, but her mother's dead. Carla and her sisters have come to visit the village where their mother grew up."

"Sisters?" Cassie asked. She couldn't believe that those other two girls were Carla's sisters. They were all so different.

"Yes, that's right. I met the youngest one just now. Her name's Po."

"Po?" Cassie said. "What kind of a nickname is that?"

"Like in the *Teletubbies*. It's short for something, but I can't remember what. She's your age, Cassie. I think she might be around tonight, if you'd like to meet her."

"I've got other plans," Cassie replied, firmly. The last thing she wanted to do was meet the sneak thief.

Back at the hotel, Cassie saw Darren from Southport. He was at Reception, asking if there were any messages from Paul. He sounded on edge.

"Are you sure there's nothing?" he repeated.

"Quite certain," the manager replied.

"What's wrong?" Cassie asked Darren.

"It's Paul. I haven't seen him since the night before last. You haven't seen him, have you?"

"No, I haven't," Cassie replied. "The last time I saw him, he was dancing with some girl."

She was going to say more, but Darren seemed relieved.

"You think he's with her?" he asked. Before Cassie could reply, he went on, "I thought Paul might be fed up with me for spending all my time with Monica."

Monica was the German girl who Darren was seeing.

"He was a bit fed up with you," Cassie said. "But it's strange if he hasn't been back to the hotel at all."

"Not that strange," Darren said. "If Paul's got off with someone, I'm not worried."

"See you, then," Cassie said and went up to her room. It was funny, she thought. Paul was an ordinary lad. Alice was older than him and very good looking. Were the two of them *really* spending all their time together? If so, maybe the couple would show up with Carla tonight.

Chapter 5
At The Beach Bar

The trouble with hanging around with two boys was that you never got properly close to either of them. If Cassie had brought a friend, the two of them could pair off with Callum *and* Nick. But she hadn't. That night, at the disco, she danced with both boys again. She liked each of them a lot.

After a while, though, they ran out of things to talk about. Nobody else asked Cassie to dance. She was clearly with Nick and Callum. Cassie tried to work out how to break the logjam. Two days ago, she would have killed to have a choice of male company. But she wanted more than company. She wanted a boyfriend. She wanted someone she could tell her friends at school about, without having to invent half of it.

At ten, Nick got up. He was going to ask her to dance again. Suddenly, Cassie was tired of the ear-splitting disco music.

"Do you fancy going somewhere else?" she asked the boys. "The Beach Bar's ten minutes' walk away. It's meant to be good."

The boys agreed. They walked there in the warm night. The music in the Beach Bar was live and even worse than the stuff at the hotel. But it was a change. Nick went to buy them all a beer.

"Don't your parents mind you leaving the hotel at night?" Callum asked.

26

"Not really. They're too busy having fun themselves. Also, I think they figure Ben will keep an eye on me."

"Where is he?" Callum wanted to know.

"I thought he was going to be here," Cassie replied.

"Hi!" called a voice from behind her. It was Cassie's brother. He wasn't alone.

"This is Carla," he said. The tall, dark haired girl was wearing shorts and a tight vest with no bra. Callum's eyes seemed to pop out of his head.

"This is my sister, Po," Carla said, introducing the dumpy girl, who wore jeans and a loose top.

"What's *Po* short for?" Cassie asked.

"It's an old Greek name, but nobody knows how to say it," Po replied.

"You're Greek?"' Callum asked.

"My father was Greek," Po replied. "My mother is American."

That was funny. Cassie could have sworn that Ben had said it was the other way round.

Nick came back with the beers and was introduced to the two girls. He gave Cassie a look to show he'd remembered what she'd said about them.

"What's Cassie short for?" Po asked Cassie.

"Cassandra, but I never use it."

"Cassandra's an old Greek name, too," Po said, with a smug smile. Then she turned to Nick. "You're cute," she said. "I'll let you buy me a drink."

Nick did as he was told.

"Do you like dancing?" he asked Po when he came back with her beer. "There's a great disco back at our hotel."

"Maybe another night," Po said.

Cassie thought she knew why Po wouldn't go to the hotel – the staff there were keeping an eye out for a sneak thief who looked just like her. Ben bought a round of drinks. Nick and Po kept talking. Ben and Carla were holding hands. There was no sign of Alice or Paul. Suddenly, Cassie had Callum to herself, which was what she'd wanted all along.

"Wanna go outside?" Callum asked. "It's too hot in here."

Outside, on the beach, it was quiet and very dark. A gentle breeze blew sand into their beer.

"Po's the one, isn't she?" Callum asked. "She's the girl you told us about who was nicking stuff at the disco. And the tall, sexy one's her sister."

"That's right," Cassie replied. "I don't dare tell Ben. There's another sister, too. A blonde called Alice. I don't know where she is tonight."

"That Po's a bit of a case. She can really knock the beer back, did you notice?"

"Yes, but Nick's keeping up with her."

"I hope she doesn't persuade Nick to do anything stupid."

"Nick seems pretty sound to me," Cassie said.

Callum shook his head. "I'm supposed to be the reliable one. That's why Nick's mum and dad brought me on holiday with them. Nick's been in trouble with the police three times this year."

"What kind of trouble?" Cassie asked.

Callum lowered his voice. "Drugs. Driving without a licence. Then there was a fight ... I don't mean to knock him. We're mates. But sometimes he goes off on one. Do you know what I mean?"

"I think so," Cassie said. She wanted Callum to kiss her, but he didn't try anything on. At half past twelve, Ben came out of the bar with Carla. He gave Cassie a drunken wave.

"What are you still doing here? Your curfew's half past eleven."

"Mum and Dad are out on the town with some couple they met last night," Cassie reminded him. "They won't notice."

Ben didn't argue. He returned to Carla. They were cuddled up in a dark corner of the bar. They were feeling each other up and talking at the same time. "No, I can't tomorrow. We're going to the other side of the island. But I'll see you when we get back."

"I hadn't realised how late it was," Callum told Cassie. "If I don't get Nick back, we'll be in big trouble."

He hurried into the bar. Cassie followed him. There was Nick, necking with Po. They looked like they would have gone on forever if Callum hadn't dragged his friend away.

On the walk back to the hotel, the fierce wind returned. Callum tried to hold Cassie's hand, but he'd left it too late. She didn't want to hold hands in front of her brother. It was not a nice walk. Nick kept going on about Po and how he was going to be 'in there'. Cassie couldn't see what he saw in her.

"Did Carla bring my baseball cap back," she asked Ben, already knowing the answer.

"I'm sorry," her brother replied. "She lost it. I'll buy you a new one, I promise."

"Forget it," Cassie snapped. "It never suited me anyway."

Her parents were still out when they got back to the hotel. Cassie went straight to bed.

Chapter 6
Three Sisters

Cassie sat next to her brother on the long bus ride the next day. Mum and Dad were three rows in front, studying the guide book. Ben got out a magazine to look at. Cassie found it hard to read on buses. She wanted to talk. But Ben wasn't interested.

"What does Carla do?" she wanted to know.

"She's a student," Ben muttered.

"So she's older than you?" Cassie asked.

"Only a few months. It doesn't matter."

"Where's she staying?"

"The girls are all staying in a flat somewhere, I think."

"Where?"

"I don't know," Ben snapped back. "What does it matter?"

He looked out of the window at the blue sea. Cassie left it a while before asking her next question.

"How old is Po?"

"I don't know," Ben replied. "Your age, I guess."

"Those two don't look much like sisters," Cassie pointed out.

"I think Carla said that she and Po have different fathers."

"And a Greek mother?" Cassie asked.

"Why are you so interested?" Ben wanted to know. "You don't seem to like Po. But you should be glad she's come along. It means you get to spend time alone with Callum, doesn't it?"

Cassie blushed. Ben went back to his magazine. Different fathers, Cassie thought. That would make sense. And hadn't Ben said before that their mother was dead? They were supposed to be here to visit her grave. But the story didn't seem to add up.

There was something weird about the three girls. Cassie remembered what the guide had said at the ruins, two days before. He'd talked about these spirits who lived in the mountains and kept stealing things. What were they called?

"There's a third sister, isn't there?" Cassie said.

"Why do you say that?" Ben wanted to know.

"Because I saw the three of them together."

"When?" Ben asked, warily.

"The other night at the hotel disco."

"What happened?" Ben sounded irritated. "You're not saying that Carla's one of the three you told me about? The ones who sneaked in without paying?"

Cassie nodded.

"And you think Po's the one who stole all the stuff?"

"Yes," Cassie said.

"You can't be serious!" Ben said.

"Dead serious," Cassie told him. "I should have mentioned it when I first saw you with Carla. Only I didn't know that she and Po were sisters, not then."

Ben became angry. "I'm not sure what you're thinking, Cassie, but you've got it wrong. Why don't you butt out of my business and enjoy your holiday? OK?"

Cassie said nothing. Maybe she had got it wrong. But she didn't trust either Po or her older sister. Not an inch.

Chapter 7

Lost in Hania

The bus rolled into Hania, which was the second biggest town on the island. It was prettier than Heraklion and less busy.

"I don't care what you say about Carla," Ben hissed to Cassie as they got off the bus. "You won't change my mind."

Change his mind about what? As they left the bus and set off, Ben hung back.

"Something wrong?" Dad asked.

"I fancy walking round on my own for a while," Ben told him. "I'll catch up with you."

"It's a big town," Dad pointed out.

"Tell you what. If I miss you, I'll meet you back here for the bus at half past six."

Mum and Dad let Ben go. Cassie trailed after her mum and dad as they ambled into the town. She felt like a spare part. Also, she was angry with Ben, going off without her.

Once they reached the leather market, though, Cassie began to enjoy herself. The Coopers ended up buying several things, a shoulder bag for Dad, a new purse and sandals for Cassie and a briefcase for Mum. All were made from the bright, polished, local leather.

After shopping, they ate an expensive lunch on the town's lovely harbour. Mum and Dad seemed determined to max out their credit cards on this holiday.

"This place is gorgeous," Dad said. "If we come back to Crete, we must stay here."

He was looking into Mum's eyes. If they came back, Cassie realised, it would be without her. They were looking forward to a time when she and Ben had left home for good. This made her feel sad and suddenly alone.

"I think I'll go for a walk on my own," she told her parents. "I'll do the same as Ben. I'll meet you at the bus station if I don't catch up with you before."

Mum and Dad gave each other a look. Clearly, they were happy to have some time alone together. However, they weren't sure about Cassie, who was still only fifteen.

"I won't do anything silly, I promise," Cassie added.

"All right, then," Mum said. "Have you enough money?" They gave her a little more cash.

Cassie set off out of the harbour. She walked up to the big hill which overlooked the town. It was covered in flowers. They must once have been bright pink, but now they were brown and ugly. Yet the view was good.

Cassie was about to walk down when she spotted a familiar figure. He was wearing blue jeans and a T-shirt. Her brother was sitting on a bench in the shade. And he wasn't alone. Cassie watched as Ben kissed Carla. One of his hands was inside her skimpy top. Carla must have come all this way to be with him. How had Carla got here when she wasn't on the bus?

Cassie walked back down the hill before they saw her, hiding her hurt feelings. She checked her watch. It was only four. She still had two and a half hours to kill before the bus left. She came upon a bookshop which sold books in English. For some reason, Cassie remembered the legend she'd been thinking about earlier. Maybe one of the books would tell her more about the Harpies. She went inside.

Cassie was in luck. There were plenty of books in English about local legends. She picked up the one which looked best. Quickly, she found the entry on *Harpies.*

There were three Harpies, she read. They were the children of the gods Titan and Elektra. The Harpies were famous for snatching things. People blamed them for anything which could not be found, especially missing children. In the later legends, the Harpies were no longer shaped like humans. Each had become a huge, scary bird with a woman's face.

Each Harpy had a name. One was called Calaeno, which meant a dark cloud. The second was called Aello, which meant a sudden wind or storm. And the third was called Podarge. Hadn't Po said her name was short for a Greek name? *Podarge* meant swift of foot. Po was certainly that. Come to think of it, the other names sounded similar – Caelano might be Carla. Aello could be Alice.

This couldn't be chance, Cassie decided. She would bet that the girls had made up their names, taking them from the legend. The names were a warning. The three girls weren't sisters. They were modern day Harpies. Even where they lived was a mystery. Maybe, like the Harpies of the legend, they lived in a cave in the mountains.

Cassie bought the book. Then she went to look for her parents. She couldn't find them, which was strange. There weren't all that many places where tourists hung out. She climbed back up the hill where she'd seen Ben and Carla earlier. They were no longer there.

She walked by endless shops, peering inside. No joy. Most were closing. It was six o'clock and only the tourist shops remained open. But there were very few tourists left in town.

Cassie wasn't sure where she was. The bus went in half an hour. She was on a side of town where she hadn't been before. The six thirty bus was the last of the day. Cassie began to panic. She couldn't think clearly. Why had she gone off on her own? The street she was on now was wide and strange to her. She walked to the end of it and still couldn't tell where she was.

Many minutes passed. Cassie seemed to be heading out of town. The only signs ahead of her were for the zoo. Was the bus station near the zoo?

"Excuse me?" Cassie spoke to a Cretan woman who was packing up her newspaper stand. "Bus station?"

The woman seemed to understand. She pointed up the street and over the way Cassie had come. Cassie checked her watch. It was six twenty-six. She began to run. At the next big road, the traffic lights turned to green as she began to cross. Cassie decided to chance it, but as she stepped into the road, her left foot caught in a drain. She fell.

Tears flooded Cassie's eyes. She'd missed the bus and was stuck in Hania with little money and not a word of Greek.

"There she is!" Ben and Carla were running down the street. "Come on, Cassie. They're holding the bus for you!"

"I got lost," Cassie said, as Ben helped her up. "Where is the bus station?"

"Just round the corner, silly," her brother replied.

A minute later, they were on the bus. Mum and Dad were bad tempered. Cassie sat by them in the front of the bus. Ben and Carla had the back seat to themselves.

"How come *she*'s here?" Cassie asked her parents.

"Carla came on the bus before ours," Mum told her. "Which is lucky for you. You see, Carla speaks a little Greek. She managed to get the bus driver to wait."

So Carla was the hero of the hour. There were questions Cassie wanted to ask, but now wasn't the time. She rested her head on her dad's shoulder and slept. She dreamt of giant birds with female faces filling caves with stolen children.

Chapter 8
Letting Go

Cassie walked back from the bus stop to the hotel on her own. Ben had gone for a drink with Carla and Mum and Dad had stopped at a restaurant for supper. Cassie wasn't hungry. She'd half hoped that there would be a note from Callum waiting for her. If he'd asked, she would have gone out with him that night. But there was no message. She had a shower and read her book of legends.

By ten o' clock, she wanted to go to sleep, but it was still too hot. She was reading on the bed when there was a knock on her door.

"Hold on." Quickly, Cassie pulled on a robe. She thought it might be Callum. But it was only her brother.

"I thought I'd check that you were OK," he said.

"I'm fine," she said, in a sullen voice, letting him in.

"I wondered if you'd changed your mind about liking Carla, now that she's helped you."

"I never said I didn't like her," Cassie replied. "Only that I didn't trust her."

"Not that baseball cap again!" Ben protested.

"*No,* I guess her losing it was an accident. Anyway, it's nice to see you happy."

"Thanks," Ben said. "You know, I get really shy round most girls. But I can talk to Carla as easily as I can talk to you. It's wonderful. We're thinking of ..." he stopped and looked at Cassie. "I'm sorry. You seem upset."

"It's nothing," Cassie replied, though a tear was forming in her eye. She was losing him. "I'm just tired."

"I'm sorry," Ben said. "I got you out of bed, didn't I? I'll let you sleep. Good night, sis."

He went. Cassie felt very alone. Growing up, she had always worshipped Ben. He was nearly three years older than her and could do no wrong. Half her friends fancied him, even though he hardly ever spoke to them. But he spoke to Cassie. They were as close as brother and sister could be. And now all that was over. He had a girlfriend who was much older than Cassie and knew things she didn't.

Soon, he would be off to university. Cassie would be left with Mum and Dad who couldn't wait to get rid of her.

Cassie couldn't sleep. She got up and stood by the window, staring at the dark mountains. The fierce wind blew, rattling the window frames and cooling the town.

Chapter 9
Mr Reliable

At breakfast the next morning, Callum asked Cassie if she'd like to go for a walk with him.

"Just you? What about Nick?"

"He's meeting Po."

Cassie asked Ben what he was planning to do.

"Carla and I are taking the bus over to the beach at Matalla. There's great swimming over there. Carla says that they've got these terrific caves, too."

Mum and Dad said they were going to spend the day taking it easy after all the walking yesterday. But they weren't sure about Cassie going out with Callum. Mum went off to consult Nick's mum.

"I don't know why she's asking Nick's mum," Cassie told Callum. "Nick's parents haven't stopped Nick from going off with Po, so they can hardly stop you from seeing me."

"Let's hope not," Callum said.

"Nick's a bit out of order, leaving you on your own."

"If a guy gets off with a girl, he's allowed to dump his mates," Callum said. "It's an unwritten rule. Doesn't that work the same for girls?"

"I guess it does," Cassie murmured.

"Don't worry about Nick's mum. She likes me. She'll probably tell your mum that I'm Mister Reliable."

Cassie's mum returned. "Nick's mum tells me that you're very responsible, Callum. I expect you to look after Cassie and bring her safely back by dinnertime."

"No problem, Mrs Cooper," Callum replied. He winked at Cassie as they left. For a moment, she thought he was going to kiss her, but just then Nick walked by. He was hand in hand with Po.

"Where are you off to?" Cassie asked them. "Matalla beach?"

"We suggested that, but my mum and dad wouldn't let me hire a scooter," Nick told them. "So we're going into Heraklion." He winked, so that they all knew this wasn't the whole truth. Cassie guessed that they'd be spending most of the day in Po's room, wherever that was.

"I really don't know what he sees in her," Callum said. "Whereas you ..." He slipped his hand into hers. They set off into Heraklion. As they walked, Cassie told Callum what she'd read about the Harpies.

"Those three sisters remind me of them," she said.

"Three?" Callum replied. "I've only met Po and Carla."

"The middle one, Alice, is the prettiest," Cassie told him. "She's not as sexy as Carla, perhaps, but she's the most beautiful. She looks like a model in a shampoo advert. Alice is so pretty she's not real."

"Interesting," Callum said. "You know, I could understand it if Nick went for a girl like Alice. But Po – she's hardly a *Page 3* girl, is she? And I've never heard her say anything interesting."

"Me neither," Cassie agreed.

"The thing is," Callum went on, "Nick's got more ... experience of girls than I have. Back home, he gets through a girlfriend a month. They're always lookers. But he's crazy about Po. They spent all day together yesterday. I felt like a spare part. But why her? It makes no sense."

"She must have something we can't see," Cassie suggested.

"Then there's your brother and Carla. Carla belongs on the cover of *Loaded*. She could have anybody she wanted. Whereas your brother's a nice guy but – no offence – hardly a huge catch. So what does Carla see in him?"

"I don't know," Cassie said.

"Still, there's one good thing about all this," Callum went on.

"What?" Cassie asked.

"When we met you, Nick and I never discussed it, but I was sure he was going to get off with you."

"Why?" Cassie asked. "Why him and not you?"

"Because you seemed to like us both. And Nick's got more nerve than I have. So he was bound to make a move first. But then Po came along and suddenly I had you to myself."

He reached towards her and they stopped walking. Cassie didn't know what to do. Should she tell Callum that she'd liked him best from the start? Or should she just let him kiss her? However, as he drew her towards him, somebody called out.

"Hey, Cassie!"

Callum looked around. "Do you know that lad over there?" he asked.

Cassie turned. It was Paul's mate Darren. He was on the other side of the street.

"Can I have a word?" Darren called.

"Sure," Cassie said.

Darren crossed the road. "You haven't seen Paul, have you?" Darren asked. "He hasn't been in our room since that disco on Saturday night."

"How would you know?" Cassie teased. "I thought you spent all your time with that German girl."

"Monica flew home on Sunday. I'm worried about Paul. His passport's gone and all his money. You don't think he got mad with me and flew home?"

"I shouldn't think so," Cassie replied. "Probably the same thing happened to him as happened to you."

"You said you saw him dancing with some girl on Saturday night," Darren reminded her. "What did you notice about her?"

"If I'm right," Cassie replied, "the girl's called Alice."

"A white girl, blonde, well built?"

"That's her," Cassie said.

"I saw him have one dance with her. She was out of his league. So I thought maybe you and him ..." Darren turned to Callum. "No offence, but Paul did tell me he liked Cassie."

"No offence taken," Callum replied.

"Nothing happened," Cassie told Darren. "We danced, that was all."

"OK," Darren said. "Please, if you see Paul, tell him I'm worried. Get him to leave a message at the hotel for me."

"I'll do that," Cassie promised. "See you."

Darren hurried off.

"So I'm not the only one who fancies you," Callum said, when they were alone.

"But that's another weird thing," Cassie said. "Darren was right. Alice *is* out of Paul's league, just like Carla is for Ben."

"Maybe they like slumming it on holiday," Callum commented.

"Are you saying that my brother's only a bit of rough?" Cassie asked.

"I wouldn't know," Callum said. "And what about me? Am I your bit of rough?"

"You seem pretty smooth to me." Cassie grinned and Callum put his arm around her waist. It felt good.

"Maybe we're getting ourselves all worked up about nothing," Callum said. "Why waste a day of our holidays worrying about people who are having fun? Why not have fun ourselves?"

"You're right," Cassie said, slipping her arm around Callum's waist. "Let's have a great day."

They walked slowly into the city. This is what I came on holiday for, Cassie thought. Forget Mum and Dad. Forget Ben. Forget the Harpies. Today, I'm going to fall in love.

Chapter 10
Romance

For the next two hours, Cassie was in heaven. Hand in hand, she and Callum explored the city. They walked down to the harbour and explored the old Turkish fort there. They ate lunch in the big square at the heart of the city. Callum pointed something out. "Look at that guy. He must be eighty if he's a day."

The old man he'd seen was a photographer. He stood in the middle of the square with a big, old, box camera on a tripod. Beside him were two plastic buckets. Cassie and Callum watched as the old man took a photo of a couple. Then he developed it in the plastic buckets and held the black and white photo up for them to see.

"We've got to have one done," Cassie told Callum. She wanted something to remember this day by.

"Yes, let's," Callum said.

When they got closer, the couple saw that the old man had a choice of frame effects to use in the photo. They chose the soppiest. The finished picture showed Callum and Cassie cuddled close, framed by a heart shape. That would be something for Cassie to show her friends at home.

Callum waved the wet photo in the air until it was dry. Then Cassie put it carefully in her purse. Only then did Callum kiss her.

It was a long kiss. It felt like the first proper kiss of Cassie's life.

"Look!" said a harsh voice. "This is what they get up to when I leave them alone." It was Nick. He was with Po and Alice. The blonde girl wore a tiny bikini top and cut off jeans. Callum stared at her. In an instant, Cassie felt rather shabby and very young. Callum, embarrassed, pulled away from her.

"What have you been up to?" he asked his friend.

"Po and I went for a swim at this quiet beach near where she's staying," he said. "But Alice came after us."

"I had to warn them about the hidden currents there," Alice explained. Her voice could have been either English or American. "Po has no sense of danger."

"Nick's like that, too," Callum told her.

"But you're not?" Alice asked, turning her full attention on Callum. "Don't you like a little danger?"

Cassie couldn't believe it. Alice was flirting with her boyfriend even though she'd just seen the two of them kissing!

"It depends what kind of danger you have in mind," Callum replied.

And Callum was playing along!

"I'll have to see what I can come up with," Alice teased.

"Excuse me," Cassie said, getting up. "I've got to get something from the shop. I'll be back in a while."

As Cassie hurried away, she heard Alice laughing. Then Callum, Nick and Po joined in. Cassie was sure they were laughing about her. How could that harpy come along and spoil everything just when it was going so well?

Chapter 11
Heartbroken

Cassie walked around the city until she'd calmed down a little. It was only natural, she thought, that Callum would be nice to Alice. She was very beautiful, after all. It didn't mean he'd forgotten how he felt about Cassie. Everything would be all right if Cassie didn't lose her nerve. She returned to the square.

For a moment, she thought that the four had gone. But they'd only moved. They were following the shade as it moved around the square. All four of them were squeezed onto a wooden bench. Nick and Po were taking it in turns to smoke a joint. None of them noticed Cassie's return.

"She's a nice kid," Cassie overheard Callum telling Alice. "And there was no-one else to hang around with, you know?"

"I know," Alice replied. "But there is now. Can you let her down gently?"

"I don't know." Callum at least had the grace to look embarrassed. "I promised her mum I'd keep an eye on her."

"But she rushed off on her own," Alice pointed out. "You can't be responsible if she goes off in a huff, can you?"

"I guess not," Callum replied.

"Po and I know this walk through the mountains. There's lots of shade. It's very romantic. We end up in a place that's very beautiful and private."

"Sounds great," Nick said.

"Is it near?" Callum asked.

"A short bus ride from here," Alice replied.

"Let's do it," Nick urged.

Cassie felt frightened. This was like a bad dream. The Harpies were taking both boys to their cave in the mountains. They would never return. She had to stop it. But how? She could run up to them now, warn them. But they'd think she was mad. Boys would be boys. At sixteen, all they cared about was sex. Callum was a nice lad. But Alice was very good looking. Cassie could hardly blame him for wanting to go with her.

"Come on, then," Nick said. "Are we going to wait any longer?"

He stood up. That was when he noticed Cassie. It was too late for her to walk away.

71

"Could I have a word with you?" she said to Callum.

"Join us," he said, moving away from Alice on the bench.

"I don't want to join you," Cassie replied. "I just want a word before you go off for a walk in the mountains."

"You shouldn't listen in on other people's conversations," Alice said, sharply. "You might hear things you'd rather not know."

"Is that right?" Cassie said. "Just tell me something. Did you get fed up with Paul?"

"I don't know who you're talking about!" Alice protested.

"A tall, black lad. Nice looking. Rather shy. Remember?"

"I think you're mixing me up with someone else," Alice argued. "Or maybe you're one of those people who love making up rumours. Callum's told us how you accused Po of stealing from your hotel."

Po gave Cassie a smug look. Callum got up. He took Cassie by the arm. She let him pull her away until they were out of earshot of the others.

"Cassie, you're over-reacting," he said.

"Am I?" Tears filled Cassie's eyes. "A few minutes ago, we were ..."

"I really like you, Cassie. But this is a holiday. Nothing serious was going to happen between me and you. Or with ..."

"With you and Alice? No, I can see that. She's the sort of girl who enjoys stealing other girls' guys and using them. There are girls like her at my school. It's all a game to them. You're going to feel such a fool when she gets fed up with you." Cassie could hear her own voice. It was shrill and ugly.

73

"You sound like a spoilt little girl," Callum told her, in a cruel voice. "I'm sorry if I've been leading you on, Cassie. I got carried away today. But I think we'd better leave it."

"So do I!" Cassie said. She pulled the photo from her purse – the lovely, romantic photo, taken less than an hour before.

"This is what I think of you!" she said, tearing the photo into little pieces.

Pieces of her heart fluttered to the ground.

Chapter 12

Missing

Half an hour later, Cassie got back to the hotel. She hurried to her room, where she cried her eyes out.

There was a knock on the door.

"Not now!" Cassie called out, thinking it was the maid.

"Cassie?" Her father's voice. "Why are you back?" He let himself into the room. "What's going on?"

"It's those ... those *Harpies.* They've stolen everything!" Cassie couldn't help herself. She spilled the whole story. She explained why she thought the three girls were thieves. Po had stolen from the hotel guests. Carla had snatched her brother. Now Alice had taken Callum from her. She told Dad about how they'd called themselves after the Harpies. She even mentioned the joint she'd seen Nick and Po smoking in the park.

"Drugs!" Dad said, suddenly alarmed. "I think I'd better tell Nick's parents about the drugs. We were just about to have lunch with them. Come with me."

Dad dragged Cassie downstairs with him. In the hotel bar, he repeated Cassie's story to Mum and Nick's parents.

"Do you know where they've gone for a walk?" Nick's dad asked.

Cassie only had a vague idea. "They said something about a cave in the mountains," she said. "I'm worried about them."

"You sound a bit hysterical to me," Nick's dad told Cassie.

Cassie's mum, however, didn't agree with him. "Suppose Cassie's right?" she said. "Suppose there's something strange about those girls? Their sister Carla is with our Ben in Matalla."

"Ben dropped a couple of hints," Cassie told them. "Like he'd decided to do something. But he wouldn't tell me what."

Now Dad looked really alarmed. "That's it," he said. "I'll hire a car. We'll go over to Matalla to fetch Ben back."

"I'll come with you," Cassie offered.

"Please stay," Nick's dad begged. "You're the only person here who can identify Po and Alice."

"I'll go with you," Mum told Dad. "You'll be all right here, won't you, Cassie?"

"I guess," Cassie said, but she was worried. The whole thing seemed to be spinning out of her control.

Soon, her parents were on their way. Nick's dad went to the police station. His mum took Cassie with her to the British Consulate, where they had a long wait.

The consulate was a grand building in the middle of Heraklion. The consul was a fat, middle-aged man. He asked Cassie for her full name and she gave it.

"So you're called Cassandra, are you? Funny how some people choose to live up to their names."

"How do you mean?" Cassie asked.

"Read your Greek legends," the consul told her. "Apollo cursed Cassandra with the power to predict the future."

"I don't understand," Cassie said. "Why did he curse her? And what's wrong with being able to predict the future?"

"He cursed her because she wouldn't sleep with him. His curse was this – while she would always predict the truth, nobody would ever believe her. Are you telling the truth, Cassandra?"

"Listen," Cassie said. "*I'm* not the one pretending to be a creature from a Greek legend. I'm just worried about my brother."

"How long has he been missing?" the consul asked.

"He's not missing as such," Cassie explained.

"So what's the fuss about?" The consul turned to Nick's mum. "But your son *has* been kidnapped?"

"Cassie said that ..." Nick's mum tried to explain what Cassie had said earlier. She explained how her son and another boy had gone off with two girls and there were drugs involved. But everything she said came out rather muddled.

"I'm afraid you're wasting my time," the consul said, sounding annoyed. "Do you know how many young people go missing – really missing – on this island? Dozens, every year. It's enough to make you believe the legend of the Harpies. But it sounds like your brother isn't missing at all, Cassandra. As for the other two boys, I suppose I'd better ring the police ..."

He went away but came back two minutes later. He spoke to Nick's mum.

"The police collected your son and his friend a few minutes ago. They were on a popular mountain path with two young women. However, your husband has taken them back to your hotel. Satisfied?"

Smugly, the man folded his arms. Nick's mum took Cassie back to the hotel.

"I've never been so embarrassed in my life," she said. "Why did you make up such a stupid story?"

Cassie had no reply.

Chapter 13
Gone

Nick and Callum were waiting in the lobby of the hotel when Cassie walked in with Nick's mum.

"What the hell did you think you were playing at?" Callum said.

"Jealous, little cow!" Nick called her. "I suppose you think you were clever. The police even searched us for drugs! Can't you tell the difference between a hand-rolled ciggie and a joint? You silly kid! I told

Callum he was wasting his time, hanging around with you. Well, I hope you're happy now!"

He stormed off. Callum, however, remained behind.

"I'm sorry I upset you," he said. "But that was a petty thing you did. Do you know who we saw after you left? That boy who spoke to us earlier. What was his name?"

"Darren," Cassie muttered.

"That's right, Darren. He'd found his mate, Paul. Seems Paul picked up an Australian girl. He'd spent the week by the beach with her. Yet, just because he had one dance with Alice, you made up this fantastic story about her kidnapping him."

"I'm sorry," Cassie snapped, "all right? I'm very sorry. I hope you and Alice are very happy together."

84

"There's no me and Alice," Callum said. "She and her friends have decided to move on."

"Friends?" Cassie said. "They said they were sisters."

"That was just a wind-up, a silly game."

"Oh, really?" Cassie said, in a sarcastic voice. "Did they make up their names, too, to be like the Harpies I told you about?"

"I don't know," Callum said. "I guess they made up the stuff about their mother, too. But I think Alice and Carla are their real names. At least they say they are."

"And Po?" Cassie asked.

"That's obvious," Callum told her. "She's been called Po since she was a kid because she looks like a teletubby, short and pudgy. It's cruel, but Po doesn't seem to mind, maybe because she's still a big hit with boys."

"I see," Cassie said.

"Anyway," Callum went on. "I'm sorry I hurt you. But you got me back. And how!"

"That wasn't what I wanted," Cassie protested, but Callum had already gone.

Cassie went up to her room. She got into bed and began throwing things around. Then she waited for her parents to come back with Ben. Matalla was a two hour drive, each way. They would be hours yet. When they returned, all three of them would be mad. Cassie had sent Mum and Dad on a wild goose chase because of her crazy, hysterical mistake.

Hours passed. Cassie grew more and more nervous. She had made such a fool of herself. She'd never be able to look anyone in the eye again. Finally, she heard a knock on her door.

It was Mum and Dad. "You were right, love. He's gone."

Dad hugged Cassie. "I'm sorry we didn't believe you. The police told us to wait here at the hotel. There'll probably be a ransom demand."

Cassie didn't agree. "I don't think Ben's been kidnapped," she said. "I think he's gone off with the Harpies of his own free will." She explained that the other two girls had said they were about to leave. "The other night, Ben hinted at something. I think Carla might have talked Ben into going with them."

"But we fly home tomorrow!" Mum pointed out. "He gets his exam results next week!"

The police came and interviewed everybody. Nick and Callum had no idea where the three girls were staying. They weren't even sure of their real names, or whether they were travelling together. Lots of ferries left Crete all the time, going to many different islands. The four of them could be anywhere. Cassie remembered the words of the consul. *Do you know how many young people go missing on this island? Dozens, every year. It's enough to make you believe the legend of the Harpies.*

What did people say about myths and legends? They may only be made-up stories, but they keep being told because they tell us things that are still true today.

On the evening before everybody was due to fly home, the British Consul came to see them in the hotel.

"It's probable," the consul told Mum and Dad, "that your son has simply gone off with this girl. He's eighteen. Even if we find him, we can't make him return if he doesn't want to."

Then he turned to Nick and Callum. "You two got mixed up with some dangerous people. At the very least, they were playing a strange game with you. I hope you'll be more careful in future. In the meantime, you owe this young lady an apology."

Callum and Nick mumbled some words as they stared at the floor.

A day later, Nick and Callum flew home. The Coopers stayed on. No ransom demand came. There was no word from Ben.

"He's probably in Athens, having a ball with his new girlfriend," the consul said.

"But he has no money," Mum pointed out.

"There are plenty of jobs in Athens," the consul said.

"He wouldn't let us worry like this," Dad argued.

"Young people can be very selfish indeed," the consul told him, in a knowing voice.

After two long weeks, Cassie flew home to start school. Mum went with her. There was no postcard from Ben waiting, no phone message – only the unopened letter with his exam results.

Dad came home in mid-September. Dad had put posters on walls and ads in the newspaper, but there were no replies. He reported that Ben, as far as the police could tell, had left Crete of his own free will. He was not listed as lost, or missing. The British Consul had promised that, if he heard anything at all, he would contact the Cooper family at once.

But he never did.

Mr and Mrs Cooper stayed in the same house for the rest of their lives in case Ben came back. He didn't.

Cassie left home when she was sixteen and never returned. She went all over the world, working as a holiday rep. Now and then, on her travels, Cassie would see someone who looked like her brother. Other times, she would spot a woman who could be Carla. When this happened, she would get excited for a moment or two. But it was never him, or her. Cassie learnt that it was better to look away. For her brother had been so cruel that, if he were still alive, she would not want to know him.

Become a Consultant!

Would you like to give us feedback on our titles before they are published? Contact us at the e-mail address below – we'd love to hear from you!

E-mail: info@barringtonstoke.co.uk
Website: www.barringtonstoke.co.uk

Barrington Stoke would like to thank all its readers for commenting on the manuscript before publication and in particular:

Peter Allen
James Allum
Martin Atkin
Jennifer Austing
Anthony Barnes
Jamie Bevan
Angie Burroughs
Shaun Cleator
Nick Clucas
Thomas Coleclough
Matthew Cooper
Dean Crefield
Jason Davies
Paul Davies
Andrew Deer
Tim Fielder
Michael Foster
Peter Hammon
Jason Hardman
Adam Harrison
Robert Haslam
Freddie Heygate
Valerie Hirst
Neil Hobson
Robert Holmes
Edward Janman
Mark Jenkins
James Johns

Ian Jones
Callum Just
Matthew James Lappin
Alice Louth
Jamie McGuinness
Pat Madden
Paul Mathieson
Anne Mean
Joseph Nelson
James O'Hara
Chris Oldham
Craig Price
Clare Partridge
Mark Richards
Julia Rowlandson
Ben Selby
Carl Smith
Matthew Stacey
Sam Standen
Aron Stenning
Luke Sully
Martin Swann
Craig Taylor
Paul Townsend
Matthew Trevellyan
Stewart Turner
Owen Vulliamy
Kelly Williams

More Teen Titles!

Joe's Story by Rachel Anderson 1-902260-70-8
Playing Against the Odds by Bernard Ashley 1-902260-69-4
To Be A Millionaire by Yvonne Coppard 1-902260-58-9
All We Know of Heaven by Pete Crowther 1-84299-032-2
Ring of Truth by Alan Durant 1-84299-033-0
Falling Awake by Viv French 1-902260-54-6
The Wedding Present by Adèle Geras 1-902260-77-5
Shadow on the Stairs by Ann Halam 1-902260-57-0
Alien Deeps by Douglas Hill 1-902260-55-4
Runaway Teacher by Pete Johnson 1-902260-59-7
No Stone Unturned by Brian Keaney 1-84299-034-9
Wings by James Lovegrove 1-84299-011-X
A Kind of Magic by Catherine MacPhail 1-84299-010-1
Clone Zone by Jonathan Meres 1-84299-009-8
The Dogs by Mark Morris 1-902260-76-7
All Change by Rosie Rushton 1-902260-75-9
The Blessed and The Damned by Sara Sheridan 1-84299-008-X

Barrington Stoke, 10 Belford Terrace, Edinburgh EH4 3DQ
Tel: 0131 315 4933 Fax: 0131 315 4934
E-mail: info@barringtonstoke.demon.co.uk
Website: www.barringtonstoke.co.uk